For Mark Meckle and all the Nashville music makers
Your Fan,
—Barb

For the women musicians and songwriters
—Renée

Renée and Barbara would like to thank:
Morgan Powell and Robbie Evans
of the Nashville Convention and Visitors Corp
and Union Station Hotel

Text Copyright © 2020 Barbara Joosse • Illustration Copyright © 2020 Renée Graef
Design Copyright © 2020 Sleeping Bear Press • All rights reserved.
No part of this book may be reproduced in any manner without the express written consent
of the publisher, except in the case of brief excerpts in critical reviews and articles.
All inquiries should be addressed to: SLEEPING BEAR PRESS™
2395 South Huron Parkway, Suite 200, Ann Arbor, MI 48104
www.sleepingbearpress.com © Sleeping Bear Press
Printed and bound in the United States • 10 9 8 7 6 5 4 3 2 1

Library of Congress Cataloging-in-Publication Data
Names: Joosse, Barbara M., author. | Graef, Renée, illustrator. | Title: Lulu & Rocky in Nashville / written by Barbara Joosse ; illustrated by Renée Graef.
Other titles: Lulu and Rocky in Nashville | Description: Ann Arbor : Sleeping Bear Press, [2020] | Series: Our city adventures ; book 3 | Audience: Ages 4-8
| Summary: "Fox kits Lulu and her cousin Rocky visit Nashville, the Music City, taking in sights like the Goo-Goo Shop, the Country Music Hall of Fame,
and the Adventure Science Center, as well as unexpected gems"— Provided by publisher. | Identifiers: LCCN 2019036856 | ISBN 9781534110656
(hardcover) | Subjects: LCSH: Nashville (Tenn.)—Guidebooks—Juvenile literature. | Children—Travel—Tennessee—Nashville—Guidebooks—Juvenile literature.
| Classification: LCC F444.N23 J66 2020 | DDC 917.68/5504—dc23 | LC record available at https://lccn.loc.gov/2019036856

THE PARTHENON

MARATHON VILLAGE

FANNIE MAE DEES PARK

A purple envelope arrives.

Dear Lulu,

Are you and Pufferson ready for four days of adventure? Rocky and Uncle Sparky will meet you at the airport in Nashville—Music City! Then head to Union Station Hotel in the band's tour bus.

Aunt Fancy

Lulu Fox

Uncle Sparky is lead singer for the band, the Jumpstarts.

Rocky's my cousin and best friend. He gets his invitation by e-mail.

I pack in a tizzy—
twirly skirts, my harmonica,
and an autograph book.

Pufferson packs *carefully*—
bandages, sunscreen,
maps, and a compass.

There's Rocky! We bear-hug and fox-box.
Then we board Uncle Sparky's tour bus.

"Welcome to Union Station Hotel!" says Miss Honey, the concierge. "Y'all look like more fun than a basket of kittens!"

Yummy color is everywhere! When I spin, it feels like a kaleidoscope. Rocky waves to us from the balcony.

Next we boppity-pop down the Honky Tonk Highway, also known as Broadway . . .

to the Wildhorse. After Rocky and I eat Nashville hot chicken, Pufferson has a tuna fish milkshake.

In two shakes of a fox's tail, we're ready to line dance.

Whee-ha!

We pick up posters for the Jumpstarts at Hatch Show Prints.

Then we look at spingle-spangle outfits at the Country Music Hall of Fame.

But I keep wondering . . . will we see a real live star? I have my autograph book ready, just in case.

We head outside, and there one IS!
A real live STAR near the Music City Walk
of Fame! She signs my autograph book.

I am starstruck.

The next morning Miss Honey helps us put our poster in the lobby.

Then we have ice cream sundaes at the Goo Goo Shop.
Scoopsy-daisy, Pufferson!

Around the corner, we cross a bridge over the Cumberland River. From there, we look at the skyscrapers. When Rocky sees the Batman Building, he says,

"Holy Foxoli, Batman!"

I take a picture for Aunt Fancy.

Then we go to Adventure Science Center.
We observe giant-Jupiter and little-Earth.
And we think: *Earth is so little and we are so small!*
What can little-we do to take care of our home?

We may be small, but we think **big** things.

The next morning, at the Musicians Hall of Fame,
Rocky riffs on a guitar, Pufferson grooves with
Ray Charles, and I jam with Ringo Starr.

Also, we find out about famous musicians
who had songs to sing and something to say.
Did they have big thoughts too?

Then we go to the
Nashville Public Library
to see a puppet show . . .

take selfies at the *WhatLiftsYou*
wings mural in the Gulch . . .

and *Athena* at the Parthenon.

At the tippy-end of the day, we do barbecue chicken wings and bowling at Pinewood Social.

Pufferson falls in love with a bowling pin.

That night we paint our day.
Rocky paints drums and I paint me,
flying with lacy wings.

Pufferson paints a bowling pin.

On our last day, we thank Miss Honey.
She says, "You darlins take the cake,"
which means she likes us. "See you at the show!"

For breakfast we have
biscuits and jam at the
Loveless Cafe . . .

then chase around the dragon at Fannie Mae Dees Park, which Nashville calls Dragon Park. The dragon has pictures all over it, like tattoos. Rocky challenges me to find the family of teeny, tiny mice.

At Bicentennial Mall, we walk to the middle of the carillon bell towers and search for the silver dot. There it is! We stand on the dot. Then we sing, *and our small voices become big!*

Suddenly, all around us, the bells begin to ring—
bing bang bong,

almost as if they heard our song,
almost as if they're applauding.

And that's when we get it! We may be small,
but *music* makes our voices loud.

AWESOME.

At last it's time for the show—
the Jumpstarts at the Ryman Auditorium!
We settle into our seats and the

band rocks out!

After the show, we call Aunt Fancy. "THANK YOU!"

Then we board the bus and wave goodbye to Miss Honey.
We wave goodbye to the music people, the Honky Tonk
Highway, planets and puppets, dragons and Goo Goos,
bowling and biscuits and bells.

We wave goodbye to Nashville . . .

and Nashville waves back.

MORE TO KNOW!

Nashville's nicknames include: Music City (because of a long history of music), the Athens of the South (because there are approximately 20 universities and colleges), and Smashville (coined when Nashville's hockey team, the Predators, went to the Stanley Cup Finals).

The **Adventure Science Center** hosts 175 interactive exhibits, including a planetarium. You can walk through an imaginary galaxy, maneuver a jet-aircraft simulator, and experience the wonders of weightlessness.

Athena represents the Greek goddess Athena. Created by sculptor Alan LeQuire, the 42-foot-tall sculpture is housed in the Parthenon, a replica of the famous Ancient Greek structure. She's covered in real gold!

The **Batman Building**, in downtown Nashville, was nicknamed because of its dark gothic design with a top that looks like Batman's mask. Its real name is the AT&T Building.

At **Bicentennial Capitol Mall State Park**, your voice becomes amplified when you stand on the marker in the middle of the carillon towers. At the top of the hour, 95 carillon bells play the song "Tennessee Waltz." Then, from nearby City Hall, the 96th bell rings, symbolizing "the government answering the call of the people."

Broadway Street is called the Honky Tonk Highway because of all the places that host live music.

The **Country Music Hall of Fame** features 800 fancy stage costumes, the instruments of famous musicians, and even Elvis Presley's custom limo.

Fannie Mae Dees Park, better known as Dragon Park, is home to a 200-foot climbable dragon created by mosaic artist Pedro Pablo Silva.

The **Goo Goo Shop** is home of Goo Goo Cluster candy and the Dessert Bar, where you can order a sundae just the way you like it. Also, you can sign up for candy school and make your own Goo Goo!

Hatch Show Prints has advertised shows by classic country music stars since 1879. The colorful woodblock prints are designed and printed right in the shop, located inside the Country Music Hall of Fame.

The famous **Loveless Cafe** bursts with country charm and good home cookin'. It's known for biscuits and jam and Nashville hot chicken.

At the **Musicians Hall of Fame & Museum**, you can sing karaoke with Ray Charles; jam with Ringo Starr; play electric keyboard, bass, and guitar onstage; and write the next big hit.

The **Nashville Public Library** has its own residential puppet troupe, Wishing Chair Productions. Inventive shows combine storytelling, puppetry, and scenery, often using Nashville's own talented musicians.

Pinewood Social is a trendy new restaurant that includes, well . . . everything! You'll discover a full restaurant, karaoke rooms, vintage bowling alleys, and even a swimming pool!

The **Ryman Auditorium** is often called the "Mother Church of Country Music" because it hosts so many country music "greats," and because it was originally a church. The audience sits in the church's original wooden pews. From 1943–1974 it was home to the Grand Ole Opry.

The **John Seigenthaler Pedestrian Bridge** is 3,150 feet long—one of the longest pedestrian bridges in the world! It crosses the Cumberland River, where you can see barges, boats, and sometimes a showboat!

The historic **Union Station Hotel** used to be a grand *train station* . . . but now it's a grand *hotel*, right in the heart of the city! Inside, you'll find sculptures, stained-glass windows, balconies, and a cozy fireplace.

WhatLiftsYou, located in the Gulch district, is a mural painted by Kelsey Montague. Inside the lacy wings are images and memories of Nashville.

The **Wildhorse Saloon** is just off the Honky Tonk Highway, and is known for barbecue, live music, and line-dancing lessons.

Next time we're in Nashville we want to: cheer for the Nashville Sounds baseball team; create our own pancakes at Pfunky Griddle; go to a show at the Grand Ole Opry; buy fancy boots at the Boot Barn; and paint our own master-piece at the Frist Art Museum.